Miss Froopy-Frou-Frou

Butch

Ahoyty-Toyty

Ahoyty-Toyty

Helen Stephens

David Fickling Books

OXFORD · NEW YORK

To Pop - the original handsome Captain.

A DAVID FICKLING BOOK

Published by David Fickling Books
an imprint of Random House Children's Books
a division of Random House, Inc.
New York

Published simultaneously in Canada by Random House of Canada Limited, Toronto.
Originally published in Great Britain by David Fickling Books, an imprint of Random House Children's Books.

www.randomhouse.com/kids

Library of Congress Cataloging-in-Publication Data is available upon request.

ISBN 0-385-75039-0 (trade)—ISBN 0-385-75040-4 (lib. bdg.)

MANUFACTURED IN CHINA

April 2004

10 9 8 7 6 5 4 3 2 1

First American Edition

Victor is a well-behaved, lovable pup and he lives with *Miss Loopy*. **Butch** is cool and bad and he lives with *Miss Froopy-Frou-Frou*.

Victor and **Butch** love holidays and this holiday was extra exciting because it was on a really big ship. **Victor** and **Butch** couldn't wait to explore.

They sniffed out the kitchens,

crept into the cabins,

wriggled through the portholes,

ran round the deck,

and leapt onto the ladies' laps.

Suddenly the Captain arrived. "Ahoyty-toyty ladies," said the Captain.

"Ahoyty-toyty Captain," giggled *Miss Loopy* and *Miss Froopy-Frou-Frou.*

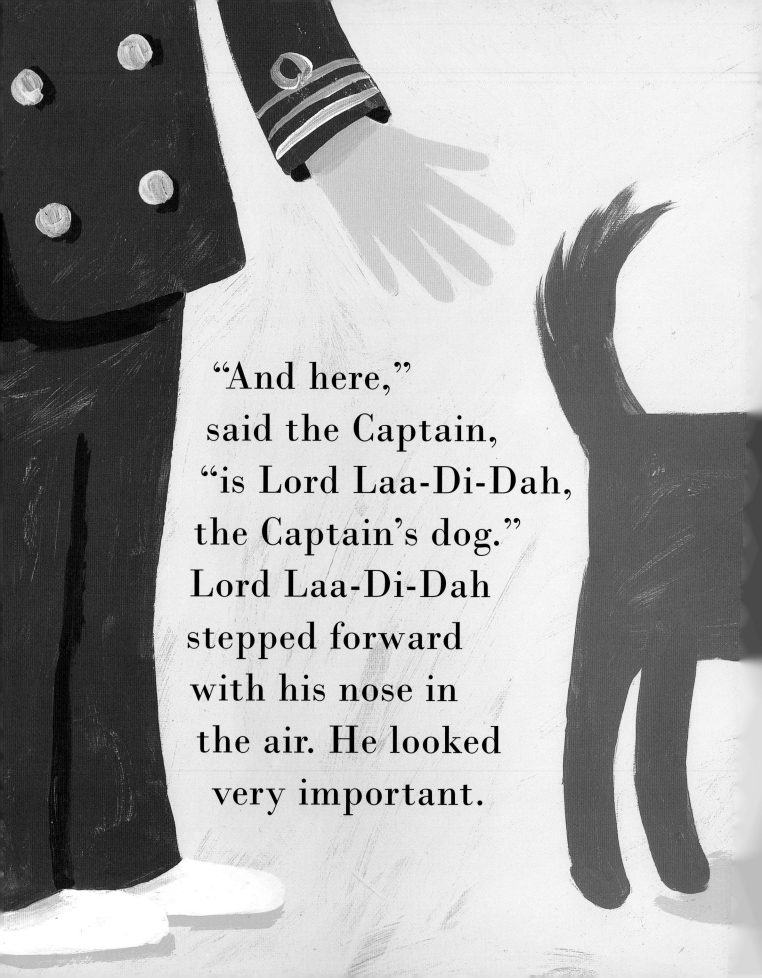

"And here,"
said the Captain,
"is Lord Laa-Di-Dah,
the Captain's dog."
Lord Laa-Di-Dah
stepped forward
with his nose in
the air. He looked
very important.

"Look at him!"
said **Butch**.
"He's fantastic!"

"Did you see how he walked with his nose in the air?" said **Butch**. "Let's practice walking like Lord Laa-Di-Dah."

"Is this right?"
said **Victor**.
"No," said **Butch**,
"it's like this."

Later **Butch** and **Victor**
saw Lord Laa-Di-Dah again.

He walked past
a pretty poodle
and he flashed her
a charming smile.
"Did you see that?"
said **Butch**.

"Let's practice our charming smiles, **Victor**," said **Butch**. "How's this?" said **Victor**. "No," said **Butch**. "It's like this."

Later they saw Lord
Laa-Di-Dah greet two
fluffy terriers.
"Ahoyty-toyty!"
said Lord Laa-Di-Dah.

"Did you hear that?" said **Butch**.
"Let's go up and say 'Ahoyty-toyty'
to Lord Laa-di-dah."
"Okay," said **Victor**.

"Ahoyty-toyty
Lord Laa-Di-Dah,"
said **Butch**.

But **Victor** got muddled.
"Asployty-bloyty!" he said.
Lord Laa-Di-Dah looked
right down his nose
at **Victor**.

"You're a useless
Captain's dog!"
said **Butch**.

Just before bedtime an invitation arrived.

Dear Butch,
Join me for dinner at the Captain's table tomorrow night.
Yours snootily,
Lord Laa-Di-Dah
P.S. wear a bow tie.

"Where's my invitation?"
said **Victor**.
But **Victor** hadn't been invited.
"Don't worry Victor darling,"
said *Miss Loopy*.
"You can sit
with me and
*Miss Froopy-
Frou-Frou*."

The next evening **Butch** walked into the dining room with his nose in the air. He was wearing a bow tie and doing his best charming smile.

Butch sat at the Captain's table and waited.

But after a while his bow tie began to itch, his face ached from the charming smile and he didn't really like the posh nosh at the Captain's table.

Still he waited.
He looked over at **Victor**
having a lovely time.
Butch felt miserable.

"Ahoyty-toyty," said Lord Laa-Di-Dah as he sat down.

"Asployty-bloyty-splithery-sployty and stick it up your snoyty!" shouted **Butch**. Then he ran straight over to his friend **Victor's** table.

"Any sausages left?"
said **Butch**.
"I saved you one,"
said **Victor**.

"Ahoyty-toyty
Victor," said
Butch.
"Asployty-bloyty
Butch,"
said **Victor**.

Butch

Victor

Miss Loopy